PIRATES of the CARIBBEAN
AT WORLD'S END

SINGAPORE!

Adapted by T.T. Sutherland

Based on the screenplay written by Ted Elliott & Terry Rossio

Based on characters created by Ted Elliott & Terry Rossio
and Stuart Beattie and Jay Wolpert

Based on Walt Disney's Pirates of the Caribbean

Produced by Jerry Bruckheimer

Directed by Gore Verbinski

Copyright © 2007 by Disney Enterprises, Inc.
All rights reserved. No part of this book may be reproduced or transmitted in any
form or by any means, electronic or mechanical, including photocopying,
recording, or by any information storage and retrieval system, without written
permission from the publisher. For information address Disney Press,
114 Fifth Avenue, New York, New York 10011-5690.

Printed in United States of America
First Edition
1 3 5 7 9 10 8 6 4 2
Library of Congress Catalog Card Number: 2006935335
ISBN-13: 978-1-4231-0379-0
ISBN-10: 1-4231-0379-3

DISNEP PRESS
New York

Chapter 1

Singapore's harbor was a busy place. Ships came in and out all day. Cargo was loaded and unloaded. Pirates walked the streets.

One man ran the town. He was a Pirate Lord named Captain Sao Feng.

Night had fallen. A pirate song drifted through the dark streets. Who was singing this song? The sound was sure to catch the attention of a pirate.

And it did. Sao Feng's second in command was a pirate named Tai Huang. He heard the song and followed it to its source. The singer was tying a boat to a dock.

It was Elizabeth Swann! She had come halfway across the world to find Sao Feng. He had something she needed.

Tai Huang told Elizabeth it was dangerous for a woman to sing that song—"especially a woman alone."

"What makes you think she's alone?" asked a voice.

Tai Huang turned around. The pirate Barbossa was standing behind him.

"Your master is expecting us," Barbossa added.

Tai Huang agreed to take them to Sao Feng. He led them to the Pirate Lord's hideout—a bathhouse.

Inside, Elizabeth and Barbossa had to give up their swords. Now they had no weapons. And they were surrounded!

Elizabeth saw that the pirates around her each had the same tattoo. The tattoo was shaped like a dragon. It meant "sworn brothers" and was the symbol of Sao Feng.

Chapter 2

Not far away, there was something moving in the water below the docks.

It looked like a line of coconuts floating past.

But under each coconut . . . was a pirate!

It was the crew of the famous dead pirate, Captain Jack Sparrow. They swam through the water. They were helping Barbossa and Elizabeth. So they could not be seen by Sao Feng's men.

They swam up to a metal grate and waited.

Squeak squeak squeak . . .

What was that sound?

It was an old woman pushing a cart. The cart was covered in birdcages.

This was not just any woman. It was Tia Dalma in disguise. Tia Dalma was a powerful mystic. She knew a lot of magic. *And* she was working with Jack's crew.

The pirates hiding in the water began to saw through the grate.

When they had made a big enough hole, the pirates slipped inside.

They were in the steam tunnels. These ran directly under Sao Feng's bathhouse. Now if there was any trouble . . . Jack's crew would be there to help.

Elizabeth and Barbossa finally met Sao
Feng. "Welcome to Singapore," he said.

"I find myself in need of a ship and a
crew," Barbossa replied.

Sao Feng knew something was going on.
That very same day, his guards had caught
a thief.

The thief had been trying to steal charts that showed the way to World's End. World's End led to Davy Jones's Locker. Was that where Barbossa wanted to go with the ship?

Sao Feng ordered his men to bring out the thief.

It was Will Turner! Elizabeth's fiancé!

Sao Feng now knew that they were all working together. But why did they want to go to World's End?

"What is it you seek?" he asked.

Will answered, "Jack Sparrow."

Sao Feng was angry. He did not like Jack. He did not want Jack to come back.

But the pirates needed Jack, Barbossa said. Jack was one of nine Pirate Lords, just like Barbossa and Sao Feng. Every Pirate Lord had to pass on his lordship before he died. Jack had not done this. There was no Pirate Lord to take his place.

Chapter 3

Right now, the Pirate Lords were needed. Why? Because a meeting of the Brethren Court had been called. The Court was made up of all nine Lords. They had to decide what to do about their biggest enemy—the East India Trading Company. Its leader, Lord Beckett, had killed many pirates. He had to be stopped.

There was one problem. Without Jack, the Court could not meet.

So Barbossa had to go to Davy Jones's Locker. He had to find Jack and bring him back. It was very important.

And Sao Feng had the charts that would lead Barbossa there.

Suddenly, Sao Feng saw something. Steng, one of his men, was standing near him. But something was wrong. Steng's dragon tattoo was melting!

It had to be a fake. Steng was not really
one of his men. He was a spy!

Sao Feng grabbed Steng. He thought
the man was working with Elizabeth and
Barbossa. Sao Feng's men pulled out
weapons.

Meanwhile, under the bathhouse, Jack's crew was worried. This looked like trouble! Quickly they passed swords up through the floor. Now Elizabeth, Barbossa, and Will were all armed, too. The pirates faced each other. Would there be a fight?

Sao Feng held a knife to Steng's throat.

"Drop your weapons, or I kill your man," he said to Barbossa and Elizabeth.

Elizabeth and Barbossa were confused. They had never seen Steng before.

Barbossa shrugged. "Kill him," he said. "He's not our man."

But if Steng was not with Sao Feng or Barbossa . . . who *was* he with?

Chapter 4

CRASH!

Men smashed through the door and windows.

Steng was working for the East India Trading Company! And now the Company agents were attacking.

All the pirates started to fight. True, pirates did not always get along. But the agents were a bigger enemy. The pirates had to stand together, or they would all die.

Swords clashed. Barbossa and Elizabeth fought bravely. Even the pirates under the floor came up to help.

In the confusion, Will and Sao Feng met in a dark corner.

They started to make a deal.

With a knife at his throat, Sao Feng agreed to give Will the charts that led to World's End. He also gave him a crew led by Tai Huang. And he gave him a ship—the *Hai Peng*. Will gave Sao Feng something, too. But Will would not tell anyone what it was.

A few minutes later, Barbossa and Elizabeth were at the docks.

Will ran up. He showed them the charts and their new ship.

All the pirates ran aboard the *Hai Peng*.

They had escaped the agents!

The *Hai Peng* quickly sailed away from Singapore. The pirates had what they had come for.

Now they were going to World's End.

They were on their way to rescue Jack Sparrow.